THE HOCKEY PLAYER'S OBSESSION

EMMA BRAY

CHAPTER
ONE

Parker

I SLAM the puck past my fellow teammate who's currently serving as the goalie in our practice session. He throws his head back and groans dramatically at his failure to block my puck.

The other forwards cheer at my victory.

I play right wing for our hockey team, and I'm damn good at what I do. I'm not being cocky, but hockey is in my blood. I don't know what I would be doing if I didn't play.

"Don't worry. I'll get you next time." The goalie points at me with his hockey stick, and I just smile.

The coach blows his whistle and gets all of our

attention. He runs down a few more essentials of our plays before calling it a day and telling us to hit the showers. I'm just getting ready to turn and do as he says when I'm stopped in my tracks by movement from the side door. The skin on the back of my neck prickles, and I turn to get a full view of the most beautiful little brunette I've ever seen.

Her dark brown locks hang down past her shoulders in luscious curls. I can see from all the way over here that her eyes are a startling hazel.

I can't stop staring at her.

My mouth is suddenly dry, and it feels like my heart rate has ticked up ten beats.

She gets closer, and I get a better look at those luminous hazel eyes framed by thick, dark lashes.

She doesn't look like she's wearing a ton of makeup, yet she has some sort of cherry red gloss on her puffy lips—they're the kind of lips a man dreams about having wrapped around his cock.

I feel myself stiffening in my pants.

"Dude," my teammate gets my attention. "Come on."

I hear him, yet I can't turn my eyes away from the beautiful brunette striding over to the coach.

I grab my teammate by the arm and nod over to her. "Who the fuck is that?"

He glances over at her, his brow furrowing. "That's

Coach Berry's daughter." My teammate gives me a quizzical look.

"He has a daughter?" My stomach sinks.

"Yeah, man, everyone knows…" my teammate says before his eyes widen in comprehension. He shakes his head and lets out a low whistle. "Look, man, I wouldn't even try it. Sure, she's beautiful, but she's the *coach's* daughter. If something didn't work out, we can't afford to lose our best right winger."

I hear what he's saying, and I comprehend the words, but I'm not processing them the way he wants me to because everything in my body is screaming that I don't give a fuck if I lose my career over this. I have to speak to this tiny angel.

I hand my hockey stick to my befuddled teammate before I start striding over to the girl who's already in a heated conversation with her dad.

"Look, I don't have time for this," he's telling her in exasperation. "Get off my back, Peyton."

"Peyton" I repeat her name.

Both Coach and the beauty turn to me simultaneously. "Parker," the coach thrusts his chin at me. "You need something, son?"

I shake my head and go for nonchalance. "Naw, just heard this was your daughter and thought I'd come over and introduce myself."

The coach beams at me approvingly as he introduces us, "Peyton, this is my best right winger, Parker Jones. Parker, my daughter, Peyton."

Peyton crosses her little arms over her chest and eyes me up and down critically. Her gaze is cutting and would normally convince me that whatever she sees leaves her lacking, but I see the slight flush that tinges her cheeks when her eyes meet mine.

I can't stop the grin that breaks across my face. "Are you a fan of the sport?" I ask her. When she doesn't answer, I go on, "You must be with the best coach in the world as your father."

Coach Berry beams at me appreciatively.

Peyton scowls, though, before she hisses, "Sports are ridiculous, especially one as stupid as hockey."

With that, she turns on her heel and stalks off the rink. I can't help but notice she's wearing a simple pair of jeans and a pink hoodie with tennis shoes, yet she somehow holds herself with the air of a girl in high heels.

"You'll have to forgive my daughter," Coach Berry apologizes for her. "She's not a fan of sports at all. Hates that my job demands so much of my time. Always has."

"Oh, it's okay, Coach." I assure him, "No offense taken."

I can't stop staring after where Peyton has already walked out the door.

No, there was definitely no offense taken because while her inexplicable hatred of sports was clear, that little blush that tinged her cheeks when our eyes met gave me hope.

She can try to deny it all she wants, but I saw the flicker in her eyes when they met mine. It reflected the same emotion reverberating through my own chest. That same feeling that made my heart skip a beat.

"Good practice today. I expect you to play like that in our game on Sunday," Coach breaks me from my thoughts.

"Yes, sir," I tell him before I head to the locker room.

I know my head should be in the game. I should be focused on our upcoming match, but the only thing I can think of now is the coach's daughter.

I don't care if the other guys say it's bad practice to try to get with the coach's daughter or that she's off limits because there's one thing I know for certain after one look into her pretty hazel eyes.

Peyton Berry is *mine*.

Peyton

I'm pissed at myself because I can't stop thinking about the cocky hockey player from yesterday.

Parker. My father's star forward.

I could see the fatherly pride gleaming in my dad's eyes as he introduced his pet player. No doubt he regards Parker as the son he never had.

What Parker doesn't know is that he's not so special. My dad does this every year. He has a player whom he singles out to be his favorite, and of course, it's usually the one who scores the most goals and makes my dad look like the best coach.

There's nothing special about Parker. This is my dad's cycle.

Never mind the fact that he has a daughter at home. All my dad cares about is hockey. So much so that it wrecked he and my mom's marriage. My dad's obsession with the sport is beyond extreme. Because of it, I had to grow up shuffling from one household to another, having two holidays—one with my mom and one with my dad. I had to put up with an asshole of a stepdad.

I wouldn't have had to do any of that if my father knew how to juggle his career and his family.

But hockey *always* came first. That's why I hate it. I hate all sports, actually. I've never been a sporty girl myself anyway.

Sports have done nothing but rip my family apart,

and I swore to myself that I would never *ever* get involved with anyone who played sports. Nothing good can come of it. Look at my mom and dad. Hockey ruined their marriage.

That's why I hate myself for that little trip I feel in my heart every time I remember Parker's icy blue eyes and dark hair.

Okay, so the guy is hot. So what? There are plenty of hot guys out there who don't play hockey.

Why does my stupid heart want to flutter around in my chest like a timid little bird when it thinks of this hockey player?

Maybe it was the way he looked at me. I don't know if anyone's ever looked at me that way before. I can't exactly describe what it was. Only that I can't get that look in his eyes out of my mind. It made me feel open and vulnerable—two things I'm not used to feeling.

It's two days later, and he keeps coming into my mind.

What pisses me off even more is when I go to sleep, I see those blue eyes of his in my dreams. I can't control my subconscious, but surely, I can control myself when I'm not asleep.

So, I keep pushing him out of my mind as I readjust the chemicals in my chemistry set.

I'm studying to be a scientist. Research has always

been my jam, and I love experimenting with new things. Who knows? Maybe I'll be the one to find the cure to cancer or something one day.

All I know is I've always been fascinated with discovering new things.

My professor lets me stay after class and gives me special access to use the lab whenever I want to work on new formulas.

Parker Jones should not be popping up in my mind right now when I'm working on this stuff.

I scowl when I realize I have just thought of his name again.

I finally properly dispose of all the toxic chemicals before washing up the set and putting everything back where it goes.

My head's not in the game right now. That thought makes me scowl too because that is such a sportsman-type phrase.

Fuck, I'm even starting to think like my dad speaks. Since when do I say "my head's not in the game"?

I huff out a breath as my stomach growls on my way out of the lab. It's way past time I refueled with something to eat, so I decide to stop at a diner by the college on my way back to my dorm.

My dad wanted me to live at home with him, but, yeah, fat chance that was happening. I moved into the dorm as soon as I could.

My mom didn't even offer to let me live with her when I went to college because it would cramp her style with my stepdad too much—and there was no way in hell I was going to live with his asshole self anyway.

Nope, having my own spot in the dorms is perfect. I've got a roommate who I hardly ever see because we're on such different schedules, and that's just fine by me. I don't get in her way, and she doesn't get in mine. We might could have even been friends, but we're both just too busy.

That's okay. I've always been fine with solitude. I'm used to being alone. My parents left me alone plenty growing up—Dad with his career and Mom looking for love with another man.

I walk into the diner and order my usual—a six-inch Italian sub. Hey, I may be tiny, but I work up quite an appetite. It seems like no matter how much I eat, I never gain any weight, so go figure. Guess I'm just lucky that way.

I'm sitting there enjoying my sub and trying not to moan like a bitch in heat at how good it tastes when a shadow suddenly towers over me.

I look up and start choking on the bite I just swallowed.

It's fucking Parker Jones.

CHAPTER
TWO

Parker

I SWEAR to God my heart stops when I see her. She looks even more beautiful than I remember.

Of course, I'm not sure I make the same impression on her because she starts choking as soon as her beautiful hazel eyes look up and meet mine.

She gulps down her bite and then picks up her drink and starts sucking on it furiously. I try not to be a typical pervert guy and notice how her cheeks hollow as she sucks on the straw.

Still, I feel my cock stiffening in my pants because damn it but I can't help associating that with how she would look with me wrapped up in her mouth.

"Are you okay, beautiful?" I ask her. I notice the way her cheeks turned pink when I address her as "beautiful."

She ignores my question and flips those gorgeous brown locks behind her shoulder. "What are you doing here?"

She scowls as I slip into the booth across from her. "The same reason you're here. Came here for a bite to eat."

She eyes me dubiously. "You came all the way to this little diner near a college campus to grab a bite to eat?"

"How do you know I don't live right up the road?"

"Do you?" she challenges.

"No," I admit with a laugh.

She doesn't laugh. Instead, she asks, "Have you ever been here before?"

"No," I tell her honestly.

"Yet you just happened to wander by," she raises her eyebrows skeptically.

"No," I'm honest once again. "I came here looking for you."

Her mouth falls open at my candor. "How did you know I come here?" she asks me suspiciously.

"I've been following you," I deadpan.

She stares at me, probably thinking I'm crazy. Hell,

maybe I am. I'm definitely something when it comes to her.

"You've been following me?" she questions in a voice like she can't believe what she really just heard.

I'm laying all my cards on the table, though. "I haven't been able to get you out of my mind since the moment I first saw you, and I'm not one to sit back, so I had to do something about that."

Her frown deepens. "So, your solution was to start stalking me?"

I tsk at her. "Stalking is such a negative term. I prefer watching."

The waiter comes over to take my order. I don't even glance at the menu. Food is the last thing on my mind, though I'm certainly hungry for something, and it's sitting right in front of me. "I'll have whatever she has."

The waiter glances at Peyton's sub before scrawling something on his pad and walking away. I've never been the jealous type, but my jaw hardens when he looks at her a beat too long. I don't like other men staring at her. I feel insanely possessive of her, which is crazy since the girl acts like I'm the last person she'd rather be sitting with right now.

When the waiter leaves, I find Peyton still staring at me dazedly. "So, you're studying to be a scientist."

She blinks in surprise. "How do you know that?"

"I asked Coach," I tell her.

Her face takes on a closed-off look at the mention of her father. I know from that reaction alone she doesn't seem to get along well with him. He had a troubled expression on his face when I asked about her too. I don't know what happened between the two of them, but the relationship between her and her father is obviously rocky.

"And you're a hockey player," she states flatly.

I don't let her prickly attitude put me off. I still see the way she blushes every time my eyes linger on her, and I feel the electric current surging between us. She has to feel it too.

I know I'm not imagining these things. This girl has put up walls, but I'm determined to break every single one of them down.

"So, what made you go into science?"

She shakes her head before she asks me in exasperation, "Parker, just what are we doing here?"

My cock presses insistently against the seam of my jeans, and every cell within my body starts buzzing at hearing my name on her lips for the first time. I want to ask her to say it again, but I already look like enough of a psycho for stalking her.

One thing I know for sure. I want to hear my name coming from her lips every day for the rest of our lives.

It doesn't matter if it's in anger or what. I just need to hear it.

I finally reach across the table to take her tiny hand in mind because I can no longer restrain myself from touching her.

Her eyes flick down to where my hand is covering hers before she looks up at me cautiously with this lost, little girl look on her face that pulls straight at my heart. Peyton might try to act all prickly and hard, but she's really a scared little girl underneath it all, and I'm ready to be her protector—anything she needs.

"I just want to get to know you. Can we do that, baby?"

Her mouth parts at the endearment, and she licks her lips.

I have to fight back a moan when I see her little pink tongue moistening her puffy flesh.

"I don't think it's a—"

I interrupt her, not willing to hear her shoot me down. I give her hand a gentle squeeze as I beg, "Please." My voice is husky and verging on desperate. I've never begged for anything in my entire life. I've always been a pretty laid-back guy, but I've never wanted anything like I want Peyton Berry.

My chest squeezes when I see her eyes soften when I say "please." My heart thumps hard as I await her verdict, not knowing if I'll be able to accept it if she says no. I'm already completely crazy about this girl.

She hesitates a moment before she finally nods and pulls her hand away from mine. "Okay, you can sit here, and we can talk until we're done eating."

I can't stop the wide smile that breaks across my face.

It's a concession, and I'll take it. I'll take anything I can get from her. I'll be in her life any way I can.

But what she doesn't know is this isn't going to stop here. I will doggedly pursue her every day until she finally gives in to what I know we both want.

Peyton Berry is *mine*.

———

Peyton

I can't believe this dude is for real. I mostly agree to let Parker stay and for us to talk over our meal just because I don't want to look like a huge bitch. Well, more of a huge bitch since I know I've already come off as a bitch to him when he's been nothing but nice to me.

He's hanging on to my every word, asking me questions about my interests, my likes and dislikes, science. He seems to truly care and find me fascinating.

And it's throwing me off because it's totally going against everything I've ever thought about self-absorbed sportsmen.

It doesn't erase the fact that he's a hockey player and I swore off any man who has anything to do with sports, but it's got me feeling all kinds of confused. I hate to admit it, but not only is Parker insanely hot, but the way he latches onto my every word is totally endearing him to me.

When he asks about my experiments and jokingly says that he'll let me experiment on him any day, my cheeks flame hotter than the sun, and that only makes him grin even wider and my heart pitter-patter even harder in my chest.

There's no doubt about it. Parker Jones is completely charming—which makes him incredibly dangerous to me because he has me rethinking what I said about swearing off sportsmen, and that's not good at all.

He might be charming, and he might seem totally into me now, but I'm sure my dad was that way with my mom when they first got together. Then, over time, sports took precedence over her.

Dad is just a coach. Parker actually plays the sport. It's his first love, and he'll always go back to it. He may think he's interested in me now, much like guys are a shiny new toy, but the newness of everything would fade and then I'd be left brokenhearted like my mom while he still has his hockey to fall back on.

Nope, that's not going to happen to me.

That's why thirty minutes after we finish eating and we're still talking, I finally catch myself and attempt to shut everything down.

"Well, look, Parker. It's been cool, but I've got class in the morning, so I really should be getting back to my dorm to go to bed."

He doesn't miss a beat. "Let me walk you," he offers as he stands from the booth.

"Oh, no, that's not necessary," I begin, but he cuts me off.

"There's no way I'm letting you walk alone, Peyton." His voice is all serious and no nonsense, like my safety really is paramount to him. "You can either let me walk with you and we can continue talking, or I'll follow behind you from a distance like a creepy stalker."

I frown at him as he towers over me with his hand held out, waiting for me to take it so he can help me from the booth.

I finally let out an incredulous huff and place my hand in his. "You really are a bit of a psycho. You know that right?"

He gives me a panty-melting, lopsided grin that makes my pulse race. "Does that mean you're going to let me walk with you?"

I roll my eyes and he chuckles, knowing that he's won this round. Dammit, I hate myself for this, but I'm fighting back my own smile at just how persistently adorable he is.

I just turned nineteen, and Parker told me he's twenty-six. He's not old by any means, but he's seven years older than me, and I suddenly feel our age gap as we walk down the street in silence with his huge form towering over my tiny one.

I hate to admit it, but this actually feels nice. I feel safe with the protective way he wraps an arm around my waist and holds me close against his side like a huge guard dog that won't let anyone or anything hurt me. A girl could get used to this.

I purse my lips and mentally check myself. I am *not* doing this. I'm not going to allow myself to fall for Parker Jones. He's a hockey player. A *hockey player*. Like my dad. He'll probably eventually be a coach like my dad when he retires from playing.

And he'll *always* choose hockey over everything else.

I don't like sports. I don't like guys who play sports. I firmly remind myself of these facts as we continue to walk in silence.

"What are you thinking about?" Parker's deep voice interrupts my thoughts.

"Nothing," I lie.

I know he knows it's a lie, but he doesn't say anything else. He lets the silence stretch between us, and I practically sigh in relief as we reach my dorm building. I turned to thank him for escorting me home, but he's having none of that. He pushes the door open and motions for me to go ahead of him.

I pause and open my mouth to say something, but he raises an eyebrow at me challengingly. His intent is clear. He's not going to let me go until he sees I'm safely inside my room, and a little part of me melts inside at that stubbornness.

I walk ahead of him, but then I think that maybe he's just doing this because he wants to know which dorm room I live in. Of course, judging by his stalk-erish behavior, he probably already knows. He admitted to watching me. I still can't believe he admitted that so freely. He's like no one I've ever met before.

We finally reach my dorm room, and I turn to him with finality. This is it. I'm not letting this go any further than here.

"Thanks for walking me home, Parker. You really didn't have to do that." I quickly turn to make my escape through the door.

He doesn't let me, though. Suddenly a palm slaps onto the door by my head, and I swallow as I feel a hand on my shoulder. He turns me around to face him, and my head tilts back to find his icy blue eyes burning down at me like twin flames.

"Peyton." The way he says my name so tenderly makes my heart crack, and I feel tears stinging at my eyes. It's ridiculous. It's stupid, and I hate myself for it. I blink them back and swallow hard.

"Don't," I whisper.

He ignores me, of course, wrapping his arms around me and pulling me flush against his hard body. My hands find their way between us, my palms flattening against his chest.

His hands spear into my hair and tilt my head up to him. His face is looming closer to me, and somewhere in the back of my mind, I'm screaming at myself that I need to tell him to stop, but it's like I'm paralyzed. I can't form the words.

My lips are already tingling in anticipation of what I know is going to happen.

And then his lips cover mine, and my knees completely buckle out from underneath me.

I am so fucked.

CHAPTER
THREE

Parker

WHEN HER HANDS fist in my shirt and she melts against me, my chest swells in victory. I feel like a warrior who's just won a battle. I have an insane urge to beat my fist on my chest like a caveman. Instead, I tighten my arms around her and hold her up as I devour the sweetness of her mouth.

I swear to God she's the sweetest thing I've ever tasted. She tastes like cherry cola, and her hair is like silk gliding through my fingertips.

She mewls into my mouth, and it damn near drives me insane.

I don't know where I get the strength to pull away

from her, but I do even though I don't want to. It's either that or take her up against the door of her dorm room, and she deserves better than that.

The first time I'm inside her is going to be on a bed where I have time to worship her like the goddess she is.

"Parker," she whispers my name in a confused voice.

I hold my hands up for her to see them. "I've never been affected by a woman this way," I confess. My hands are trembling slightly, and I see her eyes widen when she takes in her effect on me. "Look at what you do to me, baby. You've got me shaking, Peyton. What is it about you that has me all tied up in knots?"

She bites her lip and makes a whimpering noise that has me spearing my hands into her hair again. I drop my forehead onto hers and fight the urge to claim her lips once again.

I'm afraid that if I kiss her again, I won't be able to stop this. Whatever is pulsing between us is too strong, and I know she's confused and not ready for the next step.

Though I'd love nothing more than to throw her over my shoulder and cart her back to my place and never let her go, I know I can't do that. I'm going to have to earn her trust. I can't just take her captive—no matter how much I may want to.

I'm an impatient bastard, but for her, I can be patient. I take her face in my hands and look into her beautiful hazel eyes. Her lips are puffy and swollen from my kisses. "I'll see you tomorrow, beautiful," I promise her before I reach over her and open her door.

She walks inside and casts one dazed, uncertain glance back at me before she closes the door softly without a word.

I place my hand on the door and curl it into a fist, fighting to keep from opening it and going into her. It's not the right time—no matter how much I want it.

So, I go home and dream of her all night. Twice I wake up and have to stroke my hard cock off, and when the morning comes, I'm at her door bright and early.

I already have her complete class schedule memorized. Her eyes widen when she opens the door and finds me standing there. She's wearing leggings and an oversized, slouchy, off-the-shoulder sweatshirt. Her hair's hanging down her shoulders in loose waves. She doesn't have any makeup on, but she doesn't need it. Her eyelashes are naturally thick and dark, and her lips are a beautiful, natural pink. She looks so beautiful even in this casual wear. My hands twitch at my sides with the urge to pull her to me.

"Good morning, beautiful." I greet her with a grin.

She chews on her lip as she looks up at me. She

shakes her head. The walls have come back up overnight, I see. Good thing I don't mind being a bull-dozer and knocking them right back down.

"Parker, you can't keep showing up like this," she admonishes me.

"Like what? Just let me walk you to class and make sure you get there okay."

She shakes her head again, but I take her backpack from her shoulder and sling it over mine, not taking no for an answer.

Her brow pinches as she looks up at me. "I'm perfectly capable of walking myself to class."

"I know you are," I tell her. "It's not about your capability. Can't I just want to be near you?"

She chews on her lip again, and I have to fight back a groan. It's driving me insane. Finally, I warn her, "If you don't stop chewing on that beautiful lip of yours, Peyton, baby, I'm not going to be able to control myself."

She immediately releases her lip from her teeth as her mouth falls open in a shocked gasp. My cock is at full mast in my jeans. Watching her chew on her lip is so fucking erotic. Hell, everything about her is sexy. She tucks a lock of hair behind her ear, and even that turns me on.

"You're not going to let this go, are you?" she asks me.

My smile widens as I sense her resistance fading. "Not a chance, beautiful." I wink at her.

She shrugs and starts walking ahead of me, but my long stride quickly catches up to her. I place my hand on the small of her back, and while she doesn't comment on the contact, I see the blush that tinges her cheeks at the touch.

Oh yes, she can act unaffected by me, but she's just as affected by me as I am her.

She stops when we reach the door to her class and turns to me with an outstretched palm, but I ignore it and walk her into the class with her my palm still pressed on the small of her back. "Where do you sit?" I ask her.

She gives me a skeptical glance and then walks over and takes a seat near the front of the classroom. I see the surprise light her face when I plop into the seat next to her and stretch my arm out across the back of her chair.

"What are you doing?" she asks, mouth gaping.

"Sitting with you."

"But you're not in this class," she sputters.

I shrug. "Is the professor going to kick me out?"

She just shakes her head. I feel the stares of several of the female students as they undoubtedly recognize me from the ice, but I ignore them. What I'm more interested in are all the envious glances many of the male students pass our way. I make sure to give them all a hard glare and scoot my chair even closer to Peyton's so that she's wrapped securely in my body.

My message is clear. Hands off. This is *my* woman. For her part, Peyton ignores me.

The professor walks in and doesn't even act like he notices a new student in the classroom. He just goes to work on his lecture, and I can't help stealing glances at Peyton, though I do actually pay attention to the class.

I see why she's into this stuff. This science stuff is fascinating, but what's even more fascinating is watching the way her eyes light up with keen interest. I stare transfixed at the way her tiny fingers jot down notes on a pad. She has a laptop, but she doesn't pull it out like many of her fellow students. I guess she prefers to take notes the old-school way.

I love watching her pretty handwriting take form on the page. Fuck, I love everything about her. I'm completely obsessed with this girl.

I'm due to be at practice in less than an hour, but I'm seriously considering skipping it and spending my entire day shadowing her and making sure no one messes with her.

She gives me a sidelong glance when the class ends as if she's just now remembering I'm there. "Don't you have somewhere to be?" she asks me.

"Yes," I tell her honestly.

She raises an eyebrow at me. "So, shouldn't you go to wherever that is?"

"I suppose, but I'd rather stay with you, beautiful."

"I have to hit the lab," she tells me frankly, "and I'm afraid you're not allowed. Only I have special access."

I try to stop the disappointment that floods me at being separated from her but placate myself by reminding myself that I should be at practice anyway. Coach will skin me alive if I'm not there. "Okay, beautiful. I need to get to practice anyway."

And just like that, the shutters fall back on her eyes.

I immediately work to reassure her, "I'll see you as soon as practice is over."

She shakes her head. "That's really not necessary. None of this is. I don't know what you hope to accomplish here."

I run a hand through my hair in frustration. Why is she fighting me so much when I know she's feeling this too. We don't really have time to get into it now, and I don't want to leave us on a bad note, so I tuck a lock of her hair behind her ear as I promise her, "I'll see you later, and we'll talk. Okay, beautiful?"

She just shrugs like it's no big deal to her one way or the other before she flings her backpack over her shoulder and heads to the lab.

I frown after her, torn between my duty and wanting to follow her. But she's made it clear I'm not allowed in this lab or whatever, so I head to the rink where I can work out some of my aggression.

I meant what I said, though. I *will* see her later and we *will* talk. I need to straighten my girl out on a few things.

Peyton

I'M glad that he mentioned hockey and reminded me of just what he is. Still, as I work in the lab, my thoughts keep turning back to him like they did yesterday.

I'm scowling at the chemistry set again and making all sorts of errors since I can't focus on the task at hand.

Damn him for kissing me last night.

I can't get that kiss out of my head. My lips still tingle, and my cheeks heat when I think about it. I dreamed of him all night and woke up to an embarrassing moisture between my legs.

I might still be a virgin, but the way my pussy

throbbed last night lets me know that my body knows what it's meant for—and it thinks that it's meant to have Parker deep inside of it.

I press my thighs together now to ease the blooming throb in between them.

Damn it. Of all the men for me to get the hots for, why, *why* does it have to be a hockey player? And one who plays for my dad's team, no less.

I finally pack up the chemistry set after four hours of failed experiments. I sling my backpack over my shoulders and head for the door, stopping in my tracks when I find Parker standing outside of it with his shoulder leaning up against the wall.

His hair is wet like he's freshly showered, and I try to ignore the way his long-sleeved shirt stretches over his buff chest.

Damn him for having that perfect athletic body too. Damn everything about him.

"What are you doing?" I bark at him.

He doesn't even blink at my tone. He acts like I'm not being a major bitch and gives me that heart-stoppingly charming smile. "Waiting for you, beautiful. I told you I'd see you later and that we'd talk. I'm a man of my word."

"I don't want to talk," I snap at him as I start walking past him.

He ignores me of course and falls into step beside me, his strides matching mine.

"What's wrong?" he asks me as if we're a normal couple and he's trying to soothe whatever's wrong with me.

It sends me over the edge. I stop and spin on my heels to face him. I have to crane my neck up to look at his body, and that pisses me off even more. "I'll tell you what's wrong. All of this." I wave my hand between us. "You following me, inserting yourself in my life like this, acting like you care. Just stop it already."

Parker's brow furrows. "I do care. That's why I'm doing this."

He takes a step toward me, but I take a step back from him, holding my hands up. "Just back off, Parker."

He stops, his eyes flaring with heat as he looks at me stubbornly. "If I thought you meant that, I would."

"I do mean it," I huff indignantly.

"No, you don't." He shakes his head.

"Yes, I do. I think I know my own mind."

"I think you're scared to admit what this thing between us is."

I let out an incredulous laugh and run a shaky hand through my hair, his words twisting in my stomach uncomfortably. "I don't have any idea what you're talking about."

My heart flutters against my ribcage at the look on his face. He takes another step toward me, his eyes never leaving my face as he studies me closely. "I think we both know exactly what I'm talking about. Tell me your pretty little cheeks don't turn pink every time I look at you. Tell me that your heart doesn't beat away in your chest every time I'm near you. Tell me that you don't feel this electric current pulsing between us like a live wire." Parker's voice is husky, and the way he's looking at me as if he sees right through me sends my whole body into a tremor.

My breath catches, and I shake my head in denial. I can't speak the words, though, because he's right. They would be a lie.

"I feel it too." His voice is gentle as he cups my face in his hands. "It's okay, Peyton, baby. I promise you I'm right there with you. You're not alone. I feel *all* of it, plus some. I've never felt like this before, baby. I swear. And I don't know what you're so afraid of, but I vow I'll never hurt you. I'll always take care of you."

I feel those damn tears pricking at the back of my eyes, and I blink furiously to push them away. I look up into his eyes, and panic lights my chest. He's going to kiss me again, and I know that if he does, I'll do just like I did last time. I'll melt into him. I'll lose my head. There's something about Parker's lips on mine that makes me forget everything I should remember. Like how he plays hockey and how I said I'd never get involved with someone like my dad.

His head lowers toward mine, and I finally wrench myself away from him, putting distance between us. I ignore the pang I feel deep in my gut at the slightly hurt look on his face.

"Parker," my voice sounds strained. "I just can't do this. Please, leave me alone. I mean it."

With that, I clutch my backpack to my shoulder tightly and hurry away. I know that Parker could quickly catch me if he wanted to, and although I hear him call my name from behind me, I ignore him and pick up the pace.

Thankfully, he doesn't follow me. Why does that cause even more tears to spring to my eyes?

———

But of course, Parker doesn't leave me alone. He shows up the next day and somehow seems to know exactly which class is my last class of the day.

My heart does this weird thing where it both leaps and falls at the same time. I swear to god, one day him popping up like this is going to give me a heart attack. I can't handle it. All the tension and anticipation. He has my emotions all in a spin.

"What are you doing here?" I ask him as he falls

into step beside me.

He gives me a pointed look. Right, I already know what he's doing here. He's shadowing me. He already admitted it shamelessly.

"I told you I'm fine. I don't need you to walk me to and from classes."

He doesn't dignify my statements with a response. Instead, he takes my backpack and flings it over his shoulder.

"So, where do you want to eat for dinner?" he asks me like yesterday never happened.

I just look at him.

"Come on. You have to eat, Peyton. Let me take you out somewhere. You want to do something fancy or casual? I'm good with whatever."

I glance down at myself and then at him. "We're not dressed for anything fancy," I grumble.

He gives me a wide grin before he wraps an arm around my waist and starts leading me over to his vehicle, which is of course a tricked-out sports car. I would expect no less from an arrogant hockey player.

He opens the passenger side door and motions for me to get in. I don't make a fuss, knowing that there's no use denying him. He's going to get his way on this. Plus, there are too many people walking around. I don't want to draw even more attention to us than his flashy car already has. And by the way much of the female student population is tittering and giggling in groups, I would guess that they recognize him for the famous sports player he is.

That only makes me scowl even more.

I'm taken aback when Parker flings my backpack into the backseat and then bends over into the passenger seat to buckle me in. I don't think anyone has ever buckled me in before except maybe when I was a baby and don't remember it.

My cheeks are flushed at his close proximity. I smell his fresh, citrusy scent, and when he looks up, his icy blue eyes are barely an inch from my own. My breath catches, and his eyes darken as they flick down to my lips.

His breath fans over my cheek before he pulls back and walks around to the driver's side. My cheeks flame even further when I see him discretely adjust himself before he gets in.

There's something so hot about knowing that I made this big machine of a man hard. He's hard for *me*.

I fidget in my seat and try not to stare at the way his big arms flex as he throws the car into gear. Why is it sexy to see him handle a car? Are all guys hot driving, or is it just Parker?

"Where are you taking me?" I finally ask.

He doesn't answer. He just gives me a smile and a wink.

When he pulls up outside one of the fanciest restaurants in the city—one that I've never been able to eat at because you have to have a reservation booked months in advance—I start to tell him that there's no way we'll ever get in, but he's already pulling me from the car, so I stay silent, waiting for them to turn us away.

I'm shocked whenever we walk in the door and the hostess' eyes brighten as she greets Parker with a hug. I instantly stiffen. The girl is a blonde bombshell, and I wonder if he dated her before, but then I tell myself that I'm being silly, that there's no reason for me to be jealous of him.

And I'm not. I'm not jealous of him because I don't really want anything to do with him. He's just somehow attached himself onto me, and I'm just dealing with it. That's all there is to this. Once he gets bored, I'll get my life back.

I try to school my features, going for stoicism, but I must not do a good job of doing it because Parker gives me a quizzical look before he introduces me to the hostess.

Turns out she's his *sister*.

I feel like an idiot because now I see the resemblance between them. She seats us at a table by the window overlooking the water, and even though neither of us is dressed for a restaurant this fancy, I feel special at the way Parker is looking at me and the beautiful view we have. This must be one of the best tables in the house.

"So, do you have a standing reservation here or something?"

His eyes twinkle. "You could say that. My parents own the place."

I blink. Of course, I knew that Parker must have parents just like everyone else, but it never even occurred to me to ask about them or what they did.

That night we dined together, he spent the entire time asking questions about me. I didn't get to ask any about him, and I told myself that it didn't matter because I don't want to get close to him. Because he's so not my type. He plays sports, and that's all I need to know about him.

Still, I find myself asking him questions throughout dinner. I tell myself I'm just doing it to be polite, but I'm secretly interested in hearing what he has to say.

And I can't help noticing the little things he does that are so considerate. I'm sure that most people who come to a restaurant like this drink wine with their meals, yet Parker orders water with me. I'm not legally old enough to drink yet, so he doesn't drink either.

He's not audacious enough to try to order for me. He lets me pick what I want and also orders a sampler without me even asking him to so I can see what I like.

I hate to admit it, but the guy has got class. He's

sweet and thoughtful, and the way he looks at me keeps my cheeks flaming all night. He's looking at me like I'm wearing a designer dress when I'm really wearing a slouchy, off-the-shoulder sweatshirt, looking like the little coed that I am.

Even though he's just wearing a plain black tee and joggers, the way everything fits him so perfectly shows off his hard muscles. I don't think Parker could put anything on and it not show off his muscles.

I feel myself relax despite myself, and by the end of the night, I'm laughing at the jokes he keeps cracking. I know he's just doing it to see me smile, and that makes my heart trip in my chest.

By the time the evening is over with and he walks me back to my dorm, my defenses are down. I know that if he kisses me tonight, I won't resist him. In fact, I tremble at the thought of what I might let him do to me.

To my surprise, he doesn't try to kiss me. Instead, he just strokes his hand tenderly on my cheek before he places a chaste kiss on my forehead. "I'll see you tomorrow, beautiful," he tells me.

A confusing mixture of relief and disappointment swirls through me, and when I get inside my dorm room, my senses finally come crashing back in on me. It's like the fog that his presence puts me under clears.

Parker Jones is very dangerous to me, and this is

the last time I can let this happen. I *cannot* be around him again.

I slip out my phone and scroll through my contacts until I find the number I'm looking for. I type out a quick text message, already knowing what I have to do to make sure I can shut Parker Jones down once and for all.

Parker

I DREAM of her all night again. I woke up with sticky sperm staining the inside of my boxers. I haven't had a wet dream since I was a high school pup, but Peyton has me more hard-up for her than I've ever been in my entire life.

It was all I could do to wait until this morning to see her, but I frown when I quickly see that she skipped out on me early this morning.

She's pulling back from me. I know she feels this thing between us too, and it scares her for whatever reason. I don't know what that reason is, but I'm going to get to the bottom of this.

I'm not going to let her run from this. I didn't kiss her last night because I was afraid I wouldn't be able to stop if I did, but I'm burning up with my desire for her now like I've got a fever, so to hell with the consequences. The next moment I lay eyes on her, I'm going to kiss her, even if I end up fucking her in the middle of the street for all to see. Let them see. Let everyone know that she's mine only.

Her first class has already started by the time I get there, but I see her sitting in the classroom.

My frown deepens, and my chest tightens when I see the golden boy sitting next to her. His hair is blond, and he's big and buff, though not nearly as buff as me.

I don't know who this fucking prick is, but my entire body stiffens when I see him drape his arm over the back of her chair. My hands fist at my sides, and my nostrils flare.

I want to storm in there and yank him away from her, but he hasn't touched her—*yet*—so I refrain, knowing that making a scene in her class will only serve to piss her off and push her further away from me.

I stand outside the lecture hall, staring in like the psycho stalker I am and not even giving a fuck. I don't know how much time passes, but as soon as the class ends and everyone starts gathering up their books, I continue to wait outside, watching to see what this fucker is going to do and why he's with *my* Peyton.

They don't even make it to the door before he places his hand on the small of her back.

I fucking snap.

I push through the assholes coming out of the door, and I'm over to Peyton and whomever this fuckboy is in a flash. I grab his offending arm and twist it back behind his back.

"Whoa! What the fuck, dude?" he cries out as I tighten my hold on his arm.

"Don't fucking touch her." My voice is soft and deadly. I'm not the type who screams when I get angry. No, when I get really angry, like homicidal angry, I get quiet and eerily calm. And that's how I feel right now.

I have to make a conscious effort to not break this guy's arm. All I need is to go to jail and put myself further away from Peyton.

"Parker!" Her mouth falls open as she takes in me holding the dude hostage in front of her. "Let him go!"

"Who the fuck is he?" I glare at him, jealousy twisting my stomach.

"He's just a friend," she says quickly at the same time that the guy says, "Nobody, man. I'm nobody."

I let him go and shove him toward the door. "Get out of here before I change my mind and break every bone in your motherfucking body."

I ignore the stares of the students who stopped to watch all the commotion as I wrap my arm around Peyton's shoulders and pull her close against my side.

"What are you doing?" she hisses.

"This," I motion toward where the dude has already hit the door and vacated the lecture hall. "We're not doing this, baby."

Her eyes shoot fire at me, but I ignore her as I steer her out of the classroom and to my waiting vehicle. I open the door and wait for her to get in. She crosses her arms over her chest. "What if I don't want to go with you?" She juts her adorable little chin out at me stubbornly.

I feel a muscle in my jaw tick. "I am *this* close to going off, Peyton. Now is not the time to test me, beautiful. Trust me. So, get your beautiful ass in my car right now before I put you in there myself."

Her mouth falls open, and I see the pulse fluttering wildly in her neck before she huffs and finally flounces into the seat. I quickly buckle her in before closing the door and getting in the driver's side.

I don't speak to her as I slam the car into gear and take off tearing down the road.

She looks out the window before I feel her eyes cautiously on me. "Where are you taking me?"

"To my place where you belong," I grunt.

Out of the corner of my eye, I see her head swivel

completely to look at me. "What if I don't want to go with you?"

"Tough shit."

She lets out an incredulous laugh. "This is kidnapping, you know?"

I just shrug. So be it. I don't give a fuck.

"You really are insane, you know that?" she grumbles.

"So you've said," I deadpan before jealousy rears its ugly head again, and I ask the question I'm dying to know the answer to. "Do you like him?" The jealousy is evident in my tone, but fuck it. I can't help it. I'm beyond hiding it now.

She opens her mouth, but before she can speak, I remind her, "Keep in mind, you hold a man's life in your hands."

She snaps her mouth back shut before she finally admits softly, "No."

"So, you were just letting him touch you to goad me?"

She lets out a sigh before she says softly, "Parker, whatever you think is going to happen between us...it can't."

I finally pull into my driveway and throw my car into park before turning to face her fully. I cup her chin in my hand and force her eyes to meet mine. "Why are you fighting me, beautiful?"

She purses her lips together and shakes her head, dropping her eyes.

"Nu-uh, baby," I tell her stubbornly. "Don't shut me out. What is it? You can tell me, Peyton. I promise we'll work through it together."

She looks down again, but I tilt her chin back up, holding her eyes. "Peyton," I beg her, "Look at me, beautiful."

"You're a hockey player," she finally admits.

My brow furrows. "So? What does that have to do with anything?"

She takes in a deep breath before she looks at me solemnly and admits, "I don't date hockey players—or any sports players for that matter."

My frown only deepens. "Why not?"

She shakes her head and tries to look down again. "You wouldn't understand."

"Try me," I challenge her as I cup her chin again.

She takes in another deep breath before she finally says in a rush, "Because my dad is a hockey coach. He's always put hockey above everything else. It tore my family apart. He and my mom divorced because of it. I had a shitty childhood because I had to deal with a shitbag stepdad because of it. To this day, my dad will always choose hockey over me. I'm just over men who care more about sports than the women they're supposed to love. Fuck sports and the guys who play them. I don't want to get involved with someone like my dad." Her voice breaks at the end, and it tears at my heart.

I soften, and my chest hurts for her when I see the tears in her eyes. It suddenly all makes sense. These wounds her father inflicted on her have cut her deeply, and they've shaped her misconceptions about all sportsmen.

"Peyton," I say slowly, begging her to understand, "every guy who plays sports isn't like that. Yes, some guys go crazy with it, but I swear to you, beautiful, nothing will ever come before you. No career is more important than the love of my life."

Her eyes flick up to me and widen when I say the word "love." "Yeah, I know it's fast, but I fell in love with you," I tell her as I stroke her cheek tenderly. Her skin is so petal soft. She's so delicate and fragile, and it just makes me want to wrap her in my arms and never let her go. "The first moment I saw you walk onto the ice rink looking so pretty and just…" I shake my head. "I don't know. I'll never know how to properly describe what happened to me. I was captivated. I spoke to you, and you were like this fierce little kitten. Your claws came out, and you looked so adorable hissing and spitting at me. I've never felt this way about anyone before, Peyton. Don't shut me out, baby. Let me love you. It's all I want to do. I swear."

She trembles underneath my palms, and tears shine in her eyes. She's never looked more beautiful than she does in this moment, and I finally can't take it anymore.

I pull her across the seat and into my lap as I spear my hands into her hair and cover her lips with mine.

Peyton

AS SOON AS Parker's tongue parts my lips and enters my mouth, it's like fire floods my veins. I'm hot everywhere, and moisture pools between my thighs.

His hands are on my back, pressing my body flush against him, and I feel his hard length pressing up against the apex of my thighs between our clothing. And my god, he feels just as big there as he is everywhere else.

I whimper into his mouth, and he moans, his hands fisting in my hair as he deepens the kiss like he wants to devour me. He's kissing me with more passion than I've ever known in my entire life, and I'm drowning in it, and the worst thing is I don't want to be saved. I want to let my lungs fill up with his air and never come up to the shore.

He finally pulls back from me, and I gasp in air as he opens the door and lifts me. I cling to him chimp-style with my arms and legs wrapped around him. I bury my face in the crook of his neck.

I'm incapable of speaking or standing. I can't do anything but cling to him like he's my lifeline. Once he closes the door, he presses me up against the wall and claims my mouth again. I melt into him like I've done every time he kisses me. When this man kisses me, it feels like I'm coming home.

I feel like I've never felt before in my entire life, like I'm completely one hundred percent safe and cared about, and maybe I'm breaking every single one of my rules about being with a hockey player, but at this point, I don't care. I'm drunk on the feeling of his lips on mine, and I want more of it.

I'm not even fully aware of what I'm doing when I start moving my hips against his, dragging my pussy against his rock-hard erection, sending tingles shooting between my legs.

He lets out a husky moan as he places a hand on my hips. "You've got to stop doing that, baby, or I'm going to embarrass myself."

My stomach flutters at his words, and I throw my

head back as he starts kissing and licking and laving on my neck. A thousand sensations flood my entire body. I'm so intoxicated by him that I'm barely aware of how we got to the bed when he lays me on it and strips my shirt and pants from my body, leaving me in nothing but my bra and panties.

His eyes drink me in, and I fight the urge to cover myself because it's clear from the way he's looking at me that he likes what he sees.

I watch as he takes off his own clothing, leaving him in nothing but a pair of black boxers. I take in the impressive ridge of his erection straining against the material and feel a prickle of trepidation at the immense size of him.

I bite my lip as I look up at him and confess, "Parker, I've never done this before."

He goes completely still, his eyes widening slightly before he falls to his knees in front of me and takes my hands. "Are you telling me," his voice is incredulous, "that you're a virgin, Peyton?"

My cheeks flame and I try to pull my hands away, embarrassed, but he only tightens his grip on them.

I nod and swallow, licking my lips nervously. "I'm sorry."

He lets out a low chuckle before he kisses my nose reverently, never taking his eyes from me. "What are you sorry for, baby? This is the best gift anyone could have ever given me." He shakes his head, a note of wonder in his voice, "To know that no one else has ever touched you...God, it's a fucking miracle."

He kisses my lips again before he breathes in between kisses, "I am going to worship you, beautiful, and show you exactly how a man loves a woman."

Then, his lips are all over my body, on the swell of my breasts, pushing the cups of my bra down, suckling my nipples into the hot cave of his mouth, trailing down over the sensitive sides of my stomach.

And then he's in between my legs, peeling my panties off of me and kissing me in a place I never imagined I would be kissed, but, my god, it feels so fucking good.

I'm moaning and crying and arching up into him when white-hot pleasure suddenly explodes through me like a rocket ship.

I bury my hands in his hair, but he doesn't stop even when I beg him to. He keeps licking and sucking me until my eyes roll back in my head.

When I start to come back down to earth, he's completely naked. He fists the huge column of his flesh and moves between my legs, positioning himself at the juncture of my thighs.

He leans over and begins to push his thick girth into me, and I wince at the invasion. Despite the pleasure he just gave me and how soaking wet I am, it still stings. He's so big.

"Ssh," he croons soothingly. He cups my face in his big hands and looks into my eyes as he continues to push into me.

Something about seeing his icy blue gaze pinned on me calms me, and I soften beneath him.

"That's a good girl," he coaxes me. "Let Daddy in."

I go completely still at his words.

It's so fucking wrong hearing him call himself my daddy, but it causes my core to clench up, and I feel wetness gushing between us.

I whimper and bite my lip as he slides easily in the rest of the way. I feel the sting of him popping my cherry, but I'm so turned on, I hardly register the pain.

"That's right. You're Daddy's little girl, aren't you?" His eyes are blazing down at me in lust as he bottoms out inside me.

God, this is so wrong. I shouldn't like it, but my body loves it. I get even wetter when he calls himself Daddy again.

He must sense my conflicted feelings because he kisses me all over my face as he whispers in my ear, "Your father failed you, beautiful, but that's okay because your daddy is here now, and he's *never* going to let you down. I promise you this, baby."

I don't even have time to respond before he's plugging away at me, and I'm clinging to him, lifting my hips up to allow him to go deeper, needing to be as close as possible to him.

"Yes, that's it. Fuck Daddy back, baby," Parker grits out.

I feel the first flutter of something amazing happening deep inside my body, and then Parker angles his hips and hits me hard and deep one last time.

My vision blurs as I explode. "Yes, Daddy!" I scream out, clinging to him.

His breath stutters out before he roars, "Fuck, Peyton!"

Then, I feel his hot, liquid heat flooding inside me. It fills me up and then overflows, dripping between us, making a sticky mess of our sexes.

"Fuck, I'm never going to let you go, baby," he says before he buries his face in my neck and pulls me close to him, holding me off the bed with his big arms wrapped around me.

Both of our breathing is hot and heavy. When we finally catch our breath, he kisses me, and I know it's a claiming kiss. It's a kiss that possesses me heart and soul, and I know that Parker Jones has completely wrecked me. I'll never be the same again.

CHAPTER
SEVEN

Parker

"SO, my game is tonight, and I know you hate hockey, but it would really mean a lot to me if you'd be there, beautiful."

Peyton looks down and bites her lip as she stares at my chest. I'm holding her in my arms in my bed. True to my word, I haven't let her go all weekend. I've kept her wrapped up in my arms with my cock firmly planted inside her, only stopping to shower and feed her.

We haven't used protection once, and she hasn't brought it up. I don't know if it's an oversight on her part, and it might be shitty of me, but I'm not mentioning it either because I pray to God that I have gotten her pregnant. Anything it takes to tie her to me.

My dick twitches at the thought of seeing her belly swollen with my child, of letting the entire world know that she's *mine*. Only mine. My cock is going to be the only one ever inside her. I'll make damn sure of that.

I hold my breath now as I wait for her answer. I would never force her to do anything she doesn't want to do, and I don't want her to be uncomfortable, but I don't see how I'm going to be able to play without being able to look out at the crowd at my woman. I need to know where she is at all times. I need to know she's safe.

She has me wrapped around her pretty little fingers, and I don't think she even knows how bad I've got it for her.

She finally looks up at me shyly and nods.

I give her a wide smile before kissing her and slipping back inside her. She's probably sore, but she hasn't complained once, and when I try to go slow and take it easy on her, she grabs my hips and urges me to go faster.

She's incredible. Every fucking little thing about her.

I make love to her and remind her with my body and lips just how much I worship her and adore her before I finally have to drag my ass out of bed and get ready to go to all the pregame shit.

"I'll be looking for you, beautiful," I tell her right before I walk out my door, leaving her in my house.

She gives me a timid smile before she offers, "I hope you win today."

My chest swells with emotion because I know just how hard it must have been for her to say those words, seeing as how she hates sports so much. Well, she doesn't realize it, but it's not really the sports she hates so much as the fact that they took her dad away from her.

I'm actually pretty disappointed in Coach that he ever let a career take precedence over his family like that. I meant what I told Peyton. Nothing will ever come before her, and I wonder if a bit of her hesitancy is because she's still not sure if she believes it.

She's never been shown anything else, so I'm going to have to show her the truth of my words, and I'm going to do just that.

————

I'm in game mode as we prep for the match, but I can't even say that Peyton is always there in the back of my mind because she's not—she's in the front of my mind. Even in front of the game.

My eyes are constantly scanning the crowd until I finally see her. At the sight of her, the tightness that took root in my chest as soon as I left her eases.

I take in her dark blue leggings and team jersey, and my lips twitch. I don't know where she got that on such short notice, but damn. My girl looks good wearing my team's colors. My chest puffs out with pride.

She spots me and gives me a timid smile. I return it and fight the urge to skate over to the edge of the rink and pull her down for a kiss. No need to make a scene in front of Coach and the entire team. There'll be plenty of time for that later.

Coach Berry's eyes follow mine, and I watched as he does a double take, his eyes widening when he realizes it's Peyton in the stands. I don't know why he thinks she's here, but every muscle in my body goes taut as he strides over to her and begins speaking to her.

I watch closely as her face becomes guarded. I see the walls going up, and then she stands and starts stalking up the stairs. I don't know what he said to upset her, but my heart plummets within me.

Coach is fucking all of this up. I need my girl to be here. I need to be able to look at her throughout the game and know that she's safe. It's the only way I'm going to be able to play. I'm so attached to her at this point it's not even funny.

I'm already skating over to the edge of the rink where Coach is standing, still trying to talk to Peyton's receding back when I see it happen as if in slow motion.

Peyton turns around to say something to her dad, and when she does, she doesn't pay attention to what's in front of her. She trips on the edge of the stairs. My heart stops beating as her arms wave in the air for balance, and then she comes tumbling backward.

She lets out a shrill little scream of panic that pierces my heart, and the next thing I know I've yanked my skates off and jumped out of the rink to rush up to her.

I catch her just before her head slams into the bleachers. She looks up at me, tears instantly forming in her eyes. "I'm sorry, Parker," she tells me in a wobbly voice. "I can't do this."

Relief floods my chest when I see that she's not hurt. Still, I run my hands all over her, checking her ankles and legs. "Are you hurting anywhere? Does anything feel broken, beautiful?"

She shakes her head and then bites her lip as the tears trail down her cheeks. "No, but I can't stay here, Parker. I'm sorry."

I cup her face in my hands and push her hair back

from her forehead. "Shush. It's okay, baby. We don't have to. You don't have to do anything you don't want to, and I'm going to be right there beside you."

Her eyes widen. "But you've got to play. You're my dad's star forward."

I shake my head and press my lips together firmly. "Nah, fuck that. The team can get along without me for one match. If you go, I go."

Peyton wraps her little arms around my neck and burrows her head in my chest, her shoulders shaking with her silent sobs.

I scoop her up against me and turn to face Coach with icy eyes. "I'm not playing the game today, Coach. I've got to take care of my girl."

His mouth falls open as his eyes flit between us. Instead of being concerned with the fact that we're together and he knew nothing about it, he's more concerned with the game.

"Parker, come on," he tries to reason with me. He motions to Peyton. "She's not hurt. She's fine. Maybe just a little embarrassed, but she'll get over that."

Sudden anger flares up in my chest as I see first-hand that everything Peyton told me about him is true. He cares more about his career than he does his own daughter and her feelings. No wonder she resents sports so much. I can't say I fucking blame her, but I'm not going to get into it with him here. Not with all these fans watching the entire exchange.

Besides, I've got to take care of my girl. *Nothing* is more important than her.

I look at Coach Berry—a man I once admired—and shake my head in disgust before I turn and carry Peyton away with me.

I hear Coach screaming in the background, but I tune his voice out. I don't give a fuck. If they want to fire me, they can. I meant what I told Peyton. Nothing is more important to me than her.

Nothing will ever be.

EPILOGUE

Peyton

Six months later

I SMILE as I feel my husband's arms circle me. I lean back into his hold and inhale his clean, citrusy scent that I love.

Parker is amazing. Ever since that day he proved to me that he truly means what he says, the day he chose me over hockey, he just completely cemented himself in my mind. I'll never have to worry about him being like my dad and putting a career above his family. He would never do that. I know that now.

In fact, he was so pissed at my dad that I had to talk

him into going back and playing for the team again because even though I held a grudge against sports for so long, it wasn't sports that were the problem. It was my dad and his priorities, and I know that Parker is great at what he does, and he loves what he does, but his priorities are right. He loves me more. He's proved that time and time again, so I would never hold him back from what he loves doing.

And I never would have thought I'd see the day, but I attend all of his matches, sitting proudly in the sidelines and watching as my man slays out on the rink. His eyes always find mine several times throughout each game, letting me know that I'm the only reason he can get through the game, and that makes me feel so cherished and special.

I'd like to say my dad and I patched up our differences and have a good relationship now, but that would be a lie. I don't think I'll ever be able to get over how he chose his career over me and my mom my entire life, especially since he doesn't seem to have any intention of changing. He's still the same as he always was.

It is what it is, but it doesn't matter anymore because my dad might be my father, but Parker is my daddy in every way that matters.

As if he can sense what I'm thinking of, he whispers in my ear, "You make Daddy so hard, baby."

My breath hitches as he presses his hardness against my ass. He splays his hands protectively over my slightly swollen belly.

I'm just now starting to show my baby bump, and Parker loves it. He's a Neanderthal that way. He was thrilled when he found out I was pregnant, and he's already becoming overbearingly protective—even more than he usually is. I'm okay with it, though, because it shows that he really does love me and our unborn child.

"I need to finish this experiment," I tell him half-heartedly as I jot down the notes from the latest chemical I've added to my set.

"Mmm, I've got an experiment for you," he breathes directly into my ear, which he knows drives me crazy. "How long can you sit on this dick without making your daddy come?"

My core instantly clenches. My pregnancy hormones have fully kicked in because my body is always ready for Parker—even more so than usual.

Fuck the experiment.

I turn in his arms and wrap mine around his neck. He gives me that knowing, shit-eating grin as he lifts me up onto the counter, careful to stay far away from the chemistry set.

"So, what are you experimenting on this time?"

I shrug my shoulders. "I don't know. Just having a

little bit of fun." I'm always researching and learning new things, and I actually make a decent amount of money reporting my findings to scientific journals. It allows me to do what I love and stay here at home with Parker when he's not training for games, so I'm good with it for now. I'll probably work in a research lab one day, but for the time being, Parker built me my own personal home lab where I can tinker around with formulas and whatnot. He's amazing like that.

"You're going to find the cure for cancer or something equally amazing one day, baby. I just know it."

"And you're going to take home the championship this year." I smile at him.

He grins back at me, and we stare at each other for a moment, lost in each other's eyes before I can take it no longer and finally order him, "Kiss me, Daddy."

It's like I flipped a switch. Parker simply cannot handle it when I call him Daddy. I mean he really freaking loses it every time, and I love it.

He lets out a deep, guttural groan as he drags me to his chest and crashes his lips down onto mine, kissing me so deeply I feel like I'm going to suffocate. If I ever die from not having enough air because of his kisses, I'll be totally okay with that. I'll die a very happy girl.

Parker comes up right before I start getting dizzy, and then his lips are all over me. He pushes my dress up and pulls my panties to the side just as he frees his hard cock from his joggers.

I see the precum leaking out of his tip as he bobs free, and I feel more answering wetness coat the insides of my thighs as my body responds to the sight of his desire for me.

I'm so wet, he's fully seated inside me in one pump.

And of course, he comments on it too. "Beautiful baby has been sitting here dreaming of Daddy's dick," he grunts in between pumps.

I moan at his words before I lick the shell of his ear, knowing how that drives him crazy.

"Fuck," he stutters out as his hips piston in and out of me faster, jerkier.

I feel him swelling inside me and know that he's near the end. I'm right there, too. All I'm waiting for is his order.

"Come for me, beautiful," he orders me in a husky, lust-filled voice that sets my senses aflame. "Come for Daddy."

That's what sets me off. His words spoken so hotly in that deep voice of his and the way his icy blue eyes are looking down at me in adoration, the way the dark locks of his hair fall over his forehead, the sheen of sweat over his perfectly hard chest.

My vision blurs as my orgasm rips through me. I scream, and he captures my scream in his mouth, his tongue thrusting deep inside to mate with mine just as I feel his heat sear my womb.

He falls on his side and pulls me so that I'm lying on his chest.

"You're everything. You know that, baby?" he tells me as he strokes my hair back from my face.

I smile because I know he really means it. I am everything to him, and he's everything to me too.

Want more Emma Bray? Go to my website for a free book: www.authoremmabray.com.